The Killing Stroke

An Esar-Haden Tale

H. Rad Bethlen

Rooster & Raven

For the Daughters of Zeus and Mnemosyne

Author Statement Concerning Artificial Intelligence

The way I write consist of several phases.

1. Idea generation.
2. Research.
3. Story development.
4. Outlining.
5. Writing the rough draft.
6. Editing and rewriting.
7. Editing and polishing.
8. Copy editing.

I will *occasionally* use AI during the research phase if I can't locate some bit of information on my own—but I try to locate it on my own first.

I will *occasionally* use AI during the story's development if I get stuck on something—but I try to resolve my own story issues first.

I *intentionally* use AI during the copy editing phase as a stand-in for a copy editor, which I can't afford to pay for yet which I don't want to go without.

A copy editor is the last set of eyes to look at a manuscript to check for grammar, usage, spelling, and punctuation mistakes. I ask the AI copy editor to make suggestions on corrections. I evaluate those suggestions. If I agree, I make the changes.

I don't use AI for anything else.

Be comforted that this story was written by a human being for other human beings.

H. Rad Bethlen

Being superior to others is nothing other than having people talk about your affairs and listening to their opinions. The general run of people settle for their own opinions and thus never excel. Having a discussion with a person is one step in excelling him. A certain person discussed with me the written materials at the clan office. He is better than someone like me in writing and researching. In seeking correction from others, you excel them.

- *Hagakure,*
Yamamoto Tsunetomo

"One often hears it said that life means less to a dark elf than to any other race."

Esar-Haden set down the ceramic cup and at the same time dropped his other hand below the table. He slid one of his twin daggers from its sheath and held it in his lap. The hot wine sent up a pillar of steam between him and the unknown speaker. The speaker approached without a sound. That troubled the ever alert rogue, especially given how sensitive his hearing was. He looked through the steam into the face of an elderly man.

The man stood erect. His white hair framed his sun-darkened face. There was still much physical vigor in him, defying the expected infirmity of his years, but it was fading. Esar-Haden noticed that the man's hips were at a slight angle, his knees loose. This told him that the man's feet were set in a well balanced stance. The unexpected visitor wore only a simple open-front shirt and long, wide-legged pants. His tan chest was bare, hidden only by a fine coat of wiry, white hair. There was a curved blade in a scabbard at his hip. He had one hand on the hilt. His forearms were criss-crossed with scars.

Esar-Haden took this in with a glance. He also understood that even though he had a dagger free and the man's blade was sheathed, he was seated and the man had position. To act was to invite death. "Appearances are not what they seem," he mumbled, as he brought his hand above the table and set his blade down next to the cup of hot wine.

The man smiled. He moved his hand from the hilt of his sword. "May I share a drink with you?"

Esar-Haden indicated the empty bench.

"Why didn't you act?" enquired the man. "Your blade was free and I am old, hardly a threat."

"You know why."

The man nodded. A woman approached the table with a ceramic jug of wine. She set a cup before the old man. She looked into his face as she poured the steaming wine and recognized him. Her eyes grew wide. Her eyebrows rose in alarm and she hurried back to the kitchen, pulling her long skirt up with one hand, her slippered feet half-running, half-scooting.

"There is a time to act," said the man, "and a time not to act. Understanding this truth can often mean the difference between life and death."

"Both are true," said Esar-Haden.

The man nodded, thinking the dark elf had agreed with his truism, which he had. He then realized Esar-Haden had said "both." He smiled, understanding that his initial statement had been verified as well. 'Will he live up to the reputation of his race? Does life mean less to them that to all others?' The man asked himself. "You are known among the Baì."

"I've done work for them," said Esar-Haden.

"They're little more than highwaymen and street thugs."

Esar-Haden nodded. He reached to his cup and lifted it to his lips. When he set the cup down he slid his hand over to his dagger. The man watched. Esar-Haden dragged the blade across the table, lowered it out of the old man's view, and slid it back into its sheath.

"Assassin's work?" enquired the man.

Esar-Haden shook his head.

"They've not asked?" enquired the old man.

"Not allowed."

The man raised an eyebrow.

Esar-Haden downed the rest of the wine and banged his fist on the table. He glanced to the kitchen door to see if the woman was returning. He saw a man standing in the doorway, looking at their table. The woman peered from around his shoulder. Esar-Haden held up the cup. The man in the doorway spun, nearly knocking the girl over. The door shut as he disappeared into the kitchen. Esar-Haden looked back to the old man seated across from him. "Something about assassinations being out of their purview," he said. "I'm guessing some other powerful group has claimed that work."

"Perhaps," said the old man. "Would you, though? Do such work?"

"Depends—" began Esar, but he was cut off.

The door to the kitchen opened and the same woman as before came out. She carried a small rectangular tray. She hurried to the table and bowed to the old man.

"Please forgive me, Master," she said. "I am a stupid female. My slow mind did not immediately recognize you. A hundred apologies." She motioned to the tray without rising from her bent posture. "My father has made these for you and your companion. I have also brought our best wine. Please accept these offerings along with our apologies. Our humble establishment is unfit for your presence. May I pour your wine, Master?"

The man was momentarily embarrassed but recovered. "Please, rise. It is inappropriate for you to bow to me in your father's house." He looked to the woman. She did not rise but remained bent at the waist, looking to the floor. The man looked to the tray. "Yes, wine for myself and my companion."

The woman rose, picked up the ceramic jug, and poured the steaming wine with great care. She set the plate of delicacies between the two men and set two pairs of chopsticks on the rim of the plate. She then reversed course and, bent the entire time, made her way backwards through the kitchen door.

The old man turned back to Esar-Haden. "Well," he said with a frown. "I thought these peasant's clothes would disguise me."

"I still don't know who you are."

This made the old man smile.

"You, I planned to tell. It was these commoners," the man glanced around the room, "who spread gossip quicker than a dry field spreads fire," he looked back to Esar-Haden, "whom I wished to deceive." The man waved his hand. "Eh? What can one do? Gossip is gossip, one can ignore it or repeat it, one cannot stop it."

This made Esar-Haden smile. He reached out and picked up his cup, eager to taste the best wine of the establishment. "To gossip, then." The old man picked up his cup, raised it, and smiled. Both men drank. "What have you come to gossip about?"

The man picked up a pair of the chopsticks and looked over the delicacies. "Now that my presence is no doubt the topic of the house," he selected and picked up a round ball of fried dough, filled with fruit paste and covered with sesame seeds, "We'd best finish our wine and depart."

Esar-Haden picked up the other pair of chopsticks and looked from the old man to the plate. They ate and drank in silence. When the food was consumed and the jug emptied, the old man rose. He pulled a small pouch from his belt. From this he fished out a few silver coins. He tossed the coins on the table. Esar-Haden followed him outside into the evening twilight.

The old man turned and led them towards the edge of town. As the two men walked, shop keepers exited their stores to light the street lanterns. Both Esar-Haden and the old man watched to make sure they weren't followed. After both parties felt secure the old man spoke.

"My name is Vazzo." He looked to the dark elf. "A retainer to our Excellency."

"That surprises me," admitted Esar-Haden.

"Why?"

Esar-Haden pointed to the man's forearms, to the matting of scar tissue. "Nobles don't usually sport such a fine collection."

"You've a few?"

"In the off chance that my childhood hadn't provided me with ample scars," answered Esar-Haden, "my years at the military academy ensured that I reached my quota."

Vazzo laughed. "And thus you recognize the results of practice with a live blade."

Esar-Haden pulled up his sleeve to reveal similar scars. "I've not as many as your high and noble self," he said, smiling. "Perhaps I've been a quicker study than you," he added, winking to the old man.

Vazzo gave him a wry smile. "It is a pleasure to speak with one who does not always strive to kiss my behind." They walked a bit more in silence. A sombre mood overcame the old man. "There is good reason daughter and father behaved as they did. Indeed, they would have done anything I asked and were undoubtedly relieved when I left." He looked at Esar-Haden. "Not out of respect, mind you, out of fear. Long ago I founded a sword school called the School of Six Hundred Killing Strokes." He looked to Esar-Haden. "Ah, now you regard me differently."

"I've heard of your school," said Esar-Haden. "I was warned to stay away from your pupils."

Vazzo looked at him, then away. "You speak to the master."

"At least I drank some good wine before being sent to my maker."

Vazzo seemed not to register the gallows humor. "Myself and my pupils fulfill a much needed role in his Excellency's administration. It is to me he turns on the eve of battle, to ensure that victory follows. It is to me that he expresses his grievances, so that his wrath is felt. These things I am glad to do, for I have sworn my life to such endeavors." He looked to Esar-Haden. "I have built my school slowly, carefully, selecting only the most disciplined students. I cared not whose sons they were. I cared not how much gold was placed in my hand to buy admission —I tossed it away. I care only about devotion, loyalty, and discipline. My school grew in strength. We killed or absorbed our rivals. In time we were feared. I offered my services to the Emperor. Long have I fulfilled this role. Now, in my old age, I find that nothing last forever."

The lights of the town were behind the pair. A bamboo grove lie ahead, covering a small hill. Rice paddies extended to either side. Evening birds expressed their pre-slumber wishes to one another. The road turned and made its way between the fields. With the sun gone, the half moon took command of the sky. Its light transformed the long, thin bamboo leaves into miniature sparkling blades.

The man turned to face the dark elf. "While peasants fear me, my own hold me more and more in contempt," he said. "The man I thought most loyal to me has maneuvered against me. He has almost convinced the Emperor that I am a tottering old fool whose strength has left him."

"I can't imagine that," said Esar-Haden.

"You might come to believe it as my tale unfolds," said Vazzo. He became lost in contemplation. The two studied the heavens until Vazzo spoke again. "When the alpha wolf weakens, his infirmity threatens the survival of the pack. In such a situation the pack attacks him. He knows this act comes and it is his final duty to fight them and to die with honor. In this way the pack remains strong. They do not conspire behind his back, weaken him, and finally tear his throat while he sleeps." The old man clenched his fist, his face twisted in disgust. His features soon softened and he lowered his arms and splayed his fingers. "I have no male heir, only daughters. Believe me, I tried to produce a son. I have taken four wives in my time." He looked to Esar-Haden. "I do not see a daughter as less than a son. I have seen the warrior spirit manifest in both men and women." He looked away, to the darkness at the heart of the bamboo grove. "Still, I know that my pupils will not follow a woman, nor will the Emperor turn to a woman on the eve of battle." Vazzo looked at Esar-Haden. "You smile?"

Esar-Haden raised his hand, waving away any perceived insult. "Women rule my culture," he explained. "It is the males who are said to be inferior. Where I come from no woman would follow a man or turn to him on the eve of battle."

Vazzo nodded his head. He looked to the moon.

"Without a male heir my only choice was to pass my school down to my most promising student. I would marry my eldest daughter to this student. Their offspring, my grandchild, would, if born male, carry my blood and spirit and perhaps gain control of the school I've labored my entire life to establish. My school, all I have worked for, my legacy, would carry on past my death. An old man wants nothing more." Vazzo looked from the moon to the lights of the city. "I married my most dedicated pupil to my eldest. She is now pregnant with my grandchild. However, I find my wishes perverted. My pupil is not loyal, to me or my daughter. He has no respect for me, for my daughter, or for my legacy. Despite his years of tutelage under my watchful eye he has deceived me. He works to turn my pupils against me. He slanders me to the Emperor. He has subjugated my daughter to his cruel will. If he has his way he will destroy my legacy while I still live."

"Kill him." At saying this, Esar-Haden witnessed something come over the man. His shoulders slumped. He looked to the ground. "You don't think you can?"

Vazzo looked to Esar-Haden. "He is careful. He surrounds himself at all times with the best of my pupils. I poured all of my knowledge into him, treating him as my son. He is undoubtedly my equal, if not my better, for he has strength and vigor and I have old eyes and tired muscles." He looked away. "I am no longer young. I am half as fast as I once was. Age is a foe that cannot be defeated."

"You had the drop on me," observed Esar-Haden.

"Yes, I could have killed you." The man paused, then looked to the dark elf. "Might you not have also struck a killing blow?" He looked away. "I am not so certain of victory. If you had acted would I have been too slow?"

"You want me to kill your disciple?"

Vazzo looked once again to the dark elf. "You would never get close to him. It's impossible." He turned and looked to the bamboo trees. "I must choose now between my legacy and my revenge," stated Vazzo. "I fear the choice has been made for me. My legacy is lost. All that is left is my revenge." The old man paused. "He must understand my wrath. He must pay for his betrayal. I thought long and hard about how best to wound him. There seemed no way and I feared all was lost." He looked to Esar-Haden. "Finally, I understood how to strike him where he is unprotected." He lowered his head once again. "But I cannot bring myself to do it. Despite the vast number of men I have sent to their graves. Despite the fear those living have for my blade." He shook his head. The moonlight illuminated the tears running down his cheeks. "I *am* an old fool whose strength has left him." He brought his hands to his face.

"Where is he unprotected?" asked Esar-Haden. "Where could you strike?"

The old man wiped his eyes and regained his composure. He lifted his head and looked to the moon and stars. "My daughter." He looked to Esar-Haden. "I want you to kill my daughter and my unborn grandchild. If she is murdered he will lose the respect of those who now follow him. Even the Emperor will question his competence." He looked to the silver-coated leaves of the bamboo. "The greatest act of revenge is to destroy what one has created, so that he who covets it has nothing to steal."

Vazzo reached to his belt and untied his sword. He extended sword and scabbard to Esar-Haden. "This is the blade of Six Hundred Killing Strokes. I have built a school with this blade. I want you to tear it down with this blade."

It is good to carry some powdered rouge in one's sleeve. It may happen that when one is sobering up or waking from sleep, his complexion may be poor. At such a time it is good to take out and apply some powdered rouge.

- *Hagakure*,
Yamamoto Tsunetomo

Act Two

His name was Cassell and Esar-Haden followed him and his entourage for several days. He learned their patterns and habits. As the old assassin had said, Cassell was always surrounded. There were times when Vazzo's daughter was not at his side, times in which Esar-Haden could have carried out his employer's wishes. Esar-Haden did not strike. He watched and waited.

Perhaps it was some sixth sense, or perhaps it was simply a mood that came over him, but now Cassell kept Vazzo's daughter by his side at all times. Her stomach was full with child, yet she was thin in limb. She was not entirely unattractive. She had something of the old man's eyes and his wide forehead. Other than these recognizable features she had a round face, puffy cheeks, and a small mouth. She had straight, black hair cut just below the ears. She was unsteady on her thin legs, still, Cassell pulled her impatiently behind him by her wrist.

The pair, surrounded by six young, fierce-looking swordsmen from the school, passed Esar-Haden while walking up the plank ramp leading to the ferry. Several youths eyed the dark elf. He smiled and nodded to each, only to receive a sneer in reply. The ferry loaded, Esar-Haden mounting the ramp last. He glanced to the spot in the tall reeds where he had hidden his twin daggers and the old man's katana. By way of defense he had only the spells native to his people, the half-remembered spells taught to him by his former lover, Soléne, and the hand-to-hand techniques taught to him at the military academy in Pwyll. Most importantly, though, he had his wits.

Three men with long poles pushed the boat from the shore. It began its way down the river. A cold drizzle began and the passengers went below deck. They sat on mats, commoner and noble alike. There was little else in the low-ceilinged space. There were no windows. Blades of light came from between the boards above. The space was further illuminated by lanterns, the smoke finding its way out through gaps. The lanterns, which were suspended from the ceiling, swayed gently as the boat was pushed along.

A child made his way among the passengers offering rice balls and warm wine at an "affordable price." When he made a sale he rushed back to his mother to hand her the money. He did not offer one to the strange man with ebony skin, pointed ears, violet eyes, and white hair.

Cassell sat cross-legged in the center of the room, surrounded by his followers, holding his wife close to his side. He occasionally glanced at the dark elf passenger. He had never seen a dark elf. None of the passengers had. His bodyguards studied all of the ferry's occupants. They found none as threatening as Esar-Haden.

During his days of observation, Esar-Haden had seen the group take the ferry down river to a large plantation. They were accompanied by the peasants who worked the plantation's rice fields. A little outpost had grown up on the shore next to the plantation where the ferry stopped and the workers disembarked. This included a small drinking and gambling establishment. Esar-Haden was not sure what business Cassell had with the plantation's owner. Perhaps he was a relation. Or perhaps Cassell was strengthening some political tie with the rich owners. It mattered not. It didn't figure into the plan.

Cassell leaned over and spoke to one of the young men. Both Cassell and the youth were looking at Esar-Haden. The youth rose. He had to bend somewhat to avoid hitting his head on the room's low ceiling. He approached Esar-Haden, hand on the hilt of his sword. Esar-Haden felt an instinctual impulse to reach for his own daggers. He had to remind himself that his daggers, and Vazzo's sword, were well out of reach. The young man sat on his heels, knees together, in front of Esar-Haden. His hand was still on his sword.

"Who are you?"

"No one," said Esar-Haden.

"You have no name?"

"My name is Viati," lied Esar-Haden.

"What are you doing on this ferry?"

Esar-Haden chuckled. The youth frowned and tightened his grip on his sword. Esar-Haden held out his hands, palms up. "Looking for a game of skill or chance. Cards, dice, whatever comes. You play?"

"A gambler?"

"That's right," said Esar-Haden, nodding. "I like to test my luck. It thrills me." Esar-Haden lifted his chin to reveal the large black letters inked on his throat. He doubted the youth would be able to see much of them in the poor light of the below-deck room. Even if he could see the tattoo, Esar-Haden knew he would not know that it said, "Thrilled," in the dark elf language.

The youth glanced at the tattoo and then looked back into Esar-Haden's face. "Where do you come from?"

"Far to the west."

"Why have you come here?"

"I owe money everywhere else." Esar-Haden smiled. "What do you say to a game of dice? I have some on me. I'll teach you a game from my homeland."

Esar-Haden reached into his jacket. The youth's hand shot out to grab his wrist. Esar-Haden saw that another of Cassell's entourage stood and started over. The youth pulled Esar-Haden's hand free. He looked down at the pair of ivory dice held in the dark elf's long, thin fingers. The youth flung Esar-Haden's arm to the side. He kept his eyes locked onto Esar-Haden's as he reached in and searched the folds of his jacket. Finding nothing he pulled his hand back. The second youth circled around the pair and sat at Esar-Haden's back. Esar-Haden looked over his shoulder. "Sit here, eh?" He pointed to a spot in front and to the side. "I know a game for three players. You've got coin?" He looked back and forth between the youths. The first youth looked over his shoulder at Cassell, who had been listening to the entire exchange. Cassell studied Esar-Haden. The look in his eyes was one of dismissal. He looked to his wife. The youths rose and made their way back to their master.

Esar-Haden tossed the dice in the air, caught them, and stuffed them back into his interior jacket pocket. "Hey, boy," he called to the child-merchant. "I need a drink—for luck. I've got coin that's as good as anyone else's." He waved to the child. As the child cautiously approached, Esar-Haden glanced at Cassell and his men. They were no longer concerned with him and spoke amongst themselves. "Good, good," said Esar-Haden to the boy. He thought, however, of the old man's truism. This had been the time *not* to act.

. . .

Two days later Esar-Haden sat cross-legged on a pillow at the corner of a large rectangular table. A bundle containing everything he needed for the job was tucked under his legs. The table was cut away in the middle. The space was piled high with pillows. On these sat a woman in a long silk dress. She played a stringed instrument that rested in her lap. Esar-Haden had never seen such an instrument. It was something like a lute and a harp mixed together and it sounded wonderful played with such skill, as it was. The woman's back was to him. Instead of an unknown man, a dark elf no less, she chose to face a rich nobleman, one who often spent great sums on wine and women. A woman with a painted face knelt next to the nobleman, her hand in his lap.

The two men were the exclusive establishment's only patrons. The night was young, however. It had cost Esar-Haden a small fortune to bribe the host to allow him entry. He was lucky indeed to have cleaned out the gambling room down river two days prior, otherwise he would have had to come up with a different plan.

Even though he had gained entry he was treated differently than the nobleman. None of the women with painted faces came near him. The waiter had been reluctant to bring him wine or food. Finally, Esar-Haden pulled out his coin purse and stacked his silver and gold coins on the table in front of him. This brought the waiter. The painted women eyed the stack, debating.

Esar-Haden waited. He drank little wine and only nibbled at his food. He listened to the music and offered the musician some coins. She demurely accepted. In time one of the more brave, or, perhaps greedy, geisha approached. She knelt next to him and bowed her head. Esar-Haden began to coax her into conversation. He slipped coin after coin into her small, delicate hands. Soon she was talking freely, drinking the wine he bought her, and even seemed to be having a good time.

This was the scene that Cassell, his captive wife, and his six bodyguards saw when they entered the restaurant and brothel. Esar-Haden had been expecting them, although he seemed to pay them no heed. His attention, to all observers, was on the young painted woman with whom he laughed and flirted. Cassell dispatched the same two youths as before. They approached Esar-Haden from opposite sides.

"What are you doing here?" asked the same young man who had interrogated him before.

Esar-Haden halted his laughter and looked up at the young man. "Ah. You again." He laughed. "You must be good luck. Look!" Esar-Haden swung his hand out to indicate the stacks of coins. He knocked them over, feigning intoxication. The coins scattered across the table and tumbled onto the pillows. "Oops," he said to the woman, both laughing.

"I'll get them for you." She giggled. She climbed onto the table and reached into the pile of pillows, retrieving the coins. Esar-Haden reached up and patted her on the rump. He looked up to the youths.

"You're still here?" he asked, laughing. "You must want to try your luck. Eh? Dice or cards? You have coin, don't you? I'm spending mine too quickly!" Esar-Haden glanced across the room at Cassell, who was arguing with the establishment's host. The host was pointing to the coins that the young geisha was carefully stacking. She was, of course, tucking many away in the pockets and folds of her dress. Growing frustrated, Cassell waved the man away. He called to the two youths, who returned to him.

As the evening progressed the room filled with patrons. Wine flowed. Sumptuous dishes were passed around the table. The laughter and pleasurable cries of the women were heard above the music. Esar-Haden was running dangerously short of funds. His many stacks had diminished to a few lonely coins. However, the woman at his side was drunk and happy. He waved over to the host who approached.

"I must bed this woman!"

"Please, please," said the host, looking around the room at the other patrons. "This is not that kind of establishment." He bent and whispered to Esar-Haden. "This way. Follow." The host assisted Esar-Haden to his feet, reaching out to sweep the dark elf's remaining coins into his own pocket. "Come, come." Encouraged the host, leading Esar-Haden and the drunken geisha out of the room.

. . .

The woman pulled herself out of her dress, almost falling as she did so. She clung to Esar-Haden, kissed him, pulled his face into her breasts, commanded, "suck!" then collapsed onto the bed and fell asleep. Esar-Haden admired the smallness of her frame and the rise of her butt that reflected the moonlight shining through the open window. He reached out and patted her bare behind.

'Not tonight,' he thought.

He folded the blanket over the woman. He set his bundle down and unwrapped it. He stripped naked and began to apply rouge to his arms, neck and upper chest, the back of his hands and finally to his face and neck. He produced a small metal mirror from his pack and angled it in the moonlight. 'Well, you don't quite have the color of the old man, but it will fool their wine-addled minds.'

He put the container of rouge away. He set the sword aside and dressed in simple peasant clothing, similar to those that the old man had used as a disguise. He pulled a pair of shears from the pack and cut his hair to the necessary length, letting his white strands fall onto the spread cloth. He put the shears away and picked up the sword and scabbard. He drew Vazzo's sword partially free. 'A hell of a blade,' he thought, holding the Six Hundred Killing Strokes sword to the shaft of moonlight.

He found the water basin and wet a towel. He left this in the basin, setting a dry towel next to it. He set his own clothes on the bed next to the sleeping woman. He hooked his belt and daggers on the bed post. If he had to leave in a hurry he could grab them and flee. He went to the door, opened it a crack, and looked out into the hall. He looked back into the room, looking over his preparations. He noticed a chair in the corner, and went to it. He pulled it next to the door and peered back into the hall. Seeing no one he exited the room, shutting the door behind him.

He listened at the other doors in the hallway and found that "it's not that kind of establishment" was doing good business, judging from the moans of pleasure he heard. Several doors were unlocked. He cautiously but quickly explored the empty rooms. He found the one he was searching for. It was a guess, but likely choice. It was the only suite composed of two rooms, a foyer and a bedroom. If Cassell was going to indulge his passions and retain the use of his bodyguards, this would be the room. He stepped into the room and shut the door behind him.

He went to the bedroom and looked around. The room was lit only by the moonlight coming through the open window. There was a lantern on the small table. He went to it and took out the wick, tucking it into his pocket. He looked up and smiled. 'My good fortune continues,' he thought. He climbed up onto the bed, jumped up and grabbed one of the criss-crossed ceiling beams, hauled himself up, crouched, and waited.

. . .

The muscles of his calves and thighs had been screaming in agony for some time when the door to the bedroom opened and one of the youths in Cassell's entourage stepped into the room. He glanced around then stepped to the side. Cassell entered the room, dragging his wife behind him. A second woman hurried through the door before the youth exited, shutting the door behind him.

Cassell tossed his wife onto the bed. He turned as the second woman threw herself at him, kissing him, clawing at his clothes. The two, Cassell and the painted whore, began to unclothe one another. Vazzo's eldest daughter scooted up to the corner of the bed where she lie on her side, curled into a ball, holding her baby-swollen stomach with one hand, covering her face with the other, in an attempt to hide her weeping.

Cassell worked with greater effect than the prostitute. He stripped her bare while he himself stood in his pants, bare chested. He spun her around him, then pushed her onto the bed. She looked up at him. Esar-Haden felt his nerves alight. 'She's going to see me,' he thought. He began to move his hand to the hilt of the sword. He stopped when the woman looked down to Cassell's belt string.

Cassell bent and reached over the naked woman. He grabbed his wife's ankle and pulled on it. "What are you doing? Crying?" He laughed. "We've got a lively one tonight." He snorted as she pulled her ankle free of his grasp. He waved her away, returning his attention to the prostitute.

"Have I had you before?" he asked.

She shook her head, rose up to her knees, threw her arms around him and began to kiss and caress him.

Esar-Haden watched and waited.

"What do you think, wife? You could learn from her. Such passionate kisses!" He laughed. Vazzo's daughter stifled her cries. Cassell spoke to the geisha. "She's no fun, is she?"

The geisha looked at the weeping woman curled on the bed. "Does she always cry?"

"A spoiled brat. She will learn her place. Forget her," said Cassell, "now is the time for *our* pleasure to begin," he announced. "Don't look away," he said to his wife. "You must learn to behave like her." He laughed, tugging on his wife's arm. She did not turn, as he wished. She scooted as far to the edge of the bed as she could get without falling. Her swollen belly hung precariously out over the void. She held it with both hands.

Cassell and the geisha resumed their passionate kissing and caressing. Vazzo's daughter cried too loudly for her husband's patience. He bent forward and grabbed a handful of her hair. He wrenched her head to the side so he could see her face. He let go of her hair and backhanded her. Given the awkward positioning of his body the blow was not hard but it had gotten his point across. She returned to her fetal posture.

"Always complaining," he growled. He returned his attention to the paid-for-woman.

Esar-Haden unsheathed the sword. He held it pointed downwards, dipping it into the shaft of moonlight entering through the window. He angled the sword, picking up the light, reflecting onto the weeping woman's cheek. Her face was turned away and she did not notice.

As Cassell and the geisha lost themselves in passion, Esar-Haden continued to pass the shaft of reflected light over Vazzo's daughter's face, the pillow she rest her head on, and the blanket at the edge of the bed. She noticed and lifted her head to follow the unexpected movement of light.

She turned her head and sought out its source. Esar-Haden lifted the blade out of the moonlight. Vazzo's daughter searched the rafters. Her eyes finally saw the presence crouched in the darkness. Esar-Haden held a finger to his lips. He hoped that she wasn't so brainwashed as to alert her husband or worse, to call out to the swordsmen in the adjoining room.

She squinted into the darkness above her. "Father?" she mouthed.

Esar-Haden nodded his head. He lowered the sword back into the moonlight. She looked at it, recognizing it. She looked to the couple next to her in the bed. She knew her father, knew his life's work, and suspected his present purpose. She slid herself from the bed, backed up, and stood next to the window with her back to the wall. The moonlight illuminated half of her face as she looked into the rafters.

The geisha was either genuinely enjoying Cassell's attention or was putting on a fine act. She was making all the right noises at his touch. He was drawn in by her responses and had all but forgotten his wife's presence in the room.

Vazzo's daughter reached up and wiped the tears from her face. She looked to her husband and the woman he touched. She looked back to the man she mistook for her father crouching in the darkness in the rafters above. Esar-Haden motioned that she should step to the side, in front of the window. He wanted her to block as much of the feeble light as she could. Darkness was an important part of his plan.

'Any second now,' thought Esar-Haden, as he monitored Cassell's actions. He gripped the sword with both hands, balancing on the narrow beam. The geisha assisted him without knowing.

"I'm ready for you," she whispered into Cassell's ear. "I need to feel you."

"Yes, yes," said Cassell between kisses. "You cannot resist me, can you?"

"Please, hurry, I ache for you," moaned the geisha.

"See, wife," said Cassell, "this is how a real woman responds to a man's touch." He glanced at the spot where he believed his wife was curled up, weeping. He was momentarily puzzled to see only the crumpled sheet.

Esar-Haden dropped from the rafters. He landed next to the bed, driving the tip of the sword of Six Hundred Killing Strokes into Cassell's unprotected back. The sword pierced Cassell's torso, split his romance-quickened heart, exited his body, and just nicked the geisha.

Both Cassell and the woman screamed. Esar-Haden reached and covered the geisha's mouth. She looked at him, her eyes wide, then fainted, falling backwards onto the bed, Cassell's body falling on top of hers, the sword sliding free. A jet of blood shot from the wound.

Esar-Haden looked to the door. Long moments passed. The door remained closed. His sensitive ears picked up the chuckling and commentary of the youths. They had attributed the screams to something more pleasurable than dying. They took the silence in the room for two spent people, and in a way they were right.

Esar-Haden angled his head, letting his hair fall over his face. He didn't want Vazzo's daughter getting a good look at him. He felt the warmth of the blood as it washed over him. 'Perfect,' he thought. He knew that the blood would only add to the effect he hoped to have in a moment.

Cassell was dead. The geisha had fainted, or was smart enough to pretend. Either way, she wasn't a problem for the moment. That was good, he didn't want to kill her. The job wasn't over, though. Cassell's bodyguards must be dealt with. They were a necessary part of the plan, even if it required grim work to make use of them.

Esar-Haden grabbed Cassell's shoulder and slid him on top of the geisha, the blood providing ample lubrication, until his head hung over the edge of the bed. Esar paused for a moment then with a downward chop he cut off Cassell's head.

He bent and picked it up, turned, and went to the door. He paused and looked to Vazzo's daughter. She was staring at her husband's decapitated, blood-splattered corpse. Esar-Haden grunted and she looked to him. He motioned with his head that she should move to the safety of the corner. She obeyed.

The moonlight illuminated the grisly scene. Cassell's wound had sprayed blood on the walls. It ran down in rivulets. His blood dripped from the rafters. The mattress was a full sponge of blood. Excess blood pooled on its surface, ran over the edges, and dripped onto the floor. The geisha could barely be seen. What could be seen of her, her bare legs and one arm, were motionless and splattered with blood. She looked just as much a corpse as her would-be lover.

Esar-Haden turned back to the door. He reached out and knocked the butt of the hilt against the wood. The conversation in the adjoining room died down. He took a step back and to the side. He wanted the full extent of the carnage to be seen and understood. He heard the swordsmen draw their blades and gather at the door. There was a soft knock then the door opened a few inches.

"Master?" The lead youth called into the darkness of the room.

"The true master is here," growled Esar-Haden. He did his best to mimic the old man's voice.

The door opened. Esar could see one of Vazzo's treacherous pupils standing in the doorway, sword drawn. He could see the rest of the youths gathered behind him. The swordsmen peered into the room. As their eyes adjusted, they began to grasp what they saw. Looks of horror crossed their faces. Their eyes went from the bed, with its blood and bodies, to Esar-Haden, who they mistook for Vazzo. Esar-Haden lifted Cassell's decapitated head. The students looked into the vacant eyes. The eternal scream of death lingered silently on Cassell's blood-filled mouth.

Esar-Haden threw the head at them and lunged forward, screaming with rage as he did so. To them he was a wild-haired, blood-soaked spirit of vengeance. The legendary and feared sword of Six Hundred Killing

Strokes jumped out of the moonlight, a flash of steel and blood. This was enough for them. Cassell's head bounced off of the chest of the lead student. Discipline and courage fled from the group. They followed it with haste.

Esar-Haden did not follow. Instead, he knelt next to Cassell's head. He righted it, held it in place, and drove the sword down into, and through, it. The blade bit into the wood of the floor. Esar-Haden lifted the head up the length of the blade until it rested against the tsuba, the hand guard. He stood erect. He heard Vazzo's daughter step from the corner of the room.

"Father," she whispered, "You—" Esar-Haden looked over his shoulder. She was looking down at Cassell's body. "—killed." She looked to Esar-Haden, thinking he was her father.

He looked away from her. He paused for effect, then, with a growl, said, "My legacy grows within you, not his." With this he walked from the room.

He crossed the second room, exited, turned, and walked down the hall. One of the other doors opened and a man and woman, both holding their robes closed to hide their nakedness, peered out. They watched as the blood-soaked man passed. They shut the door before he could turn his murderous attention to them.

Esar-Haden looked around. All of the other doors were closed. The hall was empty, although he heard activity at the base of the stairs. He opened the door to his own room and stepped in. He knew he didn't have much time. Eventually, someone would notice that the trail of blood stopped at his door.

He jammed the chair beneath the door handle. He stripped as he crossed the room, going to the basin. He tossed the bloody clothes onto the cloth square lying on the floor. He grabbed the wet towel and began to wash himself. He heard men cautiously mounting the stairs.

They stopped at the first door, knocked, and whispered, albeit loudly, to the occupants, commanding them to leave. Esar-Haden wrung out the wet towel in the basin. He tossed it on top of the bloody clothing. He grabbed the other towel and began to dry himself, scrubbing off the last of the rouge and blood.

There was a knock at the door.

"Eh? What?" Esar-Haden called out, mimicking a sleepy voice. He looked to the slumbering woman. She did not stir.

"You must leave immediately," came a nervous voice. The knock came again. Esar-Haden could hear other men passing by his door, moving cautiously.

"Okay, okay!" called Esar-Haden. He heard the man move away from his door. He went to the bed and dressed. He rolled up the cloth and tied it. He carried the basin to the window, glanced out, and dumped the bloody water into the street below. He grabbed his belt and daggers and put them on. He tied up his hair, grabbed his bag and the roll of cloth, and went to the window. He checked the street once more. Not seeing anyone he climbed out of the window and dropped down into the street. He walked along the edge of the building, turned the corner, and stepped into an alley.

Among the words spoken by great generals, there are some that are said offhandedly. One should not receive these words in the same manner, however.

- *Hagakure,*
Yamamoto Tsunetomo

Act Three

"You did not do as I asked."

Esar-Haden set down the steaming cup of wine. He looked up and once again saw the old man staring down at him. Vazzo had no need for disguises and wore a white, crisply folded robe with elaborate embroidery. Esar-Haden followed Vazzo's bent arm to his sun-tanned and scared hand, which, gripped the hilt of the sword of Six Hundred Killing Strokes.

"Glad to see that found its way back to its proper owner," commented Esar-Haden. He looked into Vazzo's wrinkled face. The old man's emotions were hard to gauge.

"You did not do as I asked," repeated Vazzo. He tightened his grip on the hilt of his sword. He need not shift his footing, as it was already in place. The door to the kitchen opened and the woman appeared. She saw the master of the School of Six Hundred Killing Strokes, spun, and disappeared into the kitchen.

Esar-Haden searched Vazzo's eyes. He sat upright, shoulders squared. He set his hands palms down on the table. "I did the thing you would have done, had you not already admitted defeat."

A tense moment passed. Vazzo did not move, nor did Esar-Haden. Esar-Haden did not look from the old man's face to his sword, even though he feared it. The steam from the wine rose between them. A smile crept across the old man's face. His hand fell from his sword to his side. "So the master becomes a student again."

He reached into his robe and produced a leather pouch. He tossed it on the table. Esar-Haden glanced at it and then looked back to Vazzo. The old man turned and walked to the door. He stopped and half-turned. "She feels that it's a boy," he announced, smiling. "She tells me the baby swings his arms about like a wild man."

"A swordsman," countered Esar-Haden.

Vazzo looked at him. He nodded, smiled, then stepped from the common room into the evening twilight.

H. Rad Bethlen has been compared to Isak Dinesen (*Seven Gothic Tales*) and Fritz Leiber (*Swords and Deviltry*). He is known for his work in the fantasy and horror genres as well as his non-fiction. He has been published in Europe and America.

Enjoy the story?

If you liked what you read, please take a moment to **leave a review on Amazon**! Your feedback helps other readers find this story. It only takes a minute but it makes a huge difference. The Amazon algorithm requires 30-50 reviews before it will pick this book up and promote it to like-minded readers. Your review is instrumental in helping that happen!

For more great fiction and non-fiction please visit:

roosterandravenpublishing.com

hradbethlen.com

or H. Rad Bethlen's Amazon page.

www.ingramcontent.com/pod-product-compliance
Lightning Source LLC
Chambersburg PA
CBHW071228130626
46555CB00004B/1893